THE SESAME STREET PET SHOW

By Emily Perl Kingsley
Illustrated by Maggie Swanson

A SESAME STREET/READER'S DIGEST KIDS BOOK

Published by Reader's Digest Young Families, Inc.,
in cooperation with Children's Television Workshop

It was the day of Sesame Street's big pet
show. Ernie was on his way to the show,
clutching a brown paper bag, when he
saw Bert standing on the street corner.

"Come down here, Bernice. Come down!"
called Bert to his pet pigeon. "I want to
straighten out your beautiful feathers so
you'll look your best."

Bernice landed on Bert's hand and cooed happily as he smoothed her feathers. "Listen to her, Ernie," said Bert. "Isn't her cooing just music to your ears? She is sure to win the prize. Hey, Ernie, where is *your* pet?"

"He's right here, Bert, right inside this paper bag. But you can't see him until the show," said Ernie. "I want him to be a surprise. See you later, Bert."

Ernie walked down Sesame Street and passed
Big Bird, who was talking into a fishbowl. "That's
right, Goldie, another few laps," Big Bird said to his
pet fish, who was swimming furiously back and
forth in the bowl. "I bet no other pet at the show will
be able to swim as fast as you can. You're sure to win
the prize."

Ernie held up his bag. "My pet can't swim," said
Ernie, "but he's going to win the prize, anyway."

"Hey, Ernie," said Cookie Monster, who was standing with a parrot on his shoulder. "Me have *talking* pet for pet show. Patricia the Parrot get prize at show!"

"Patricia want a cookie," said the parrot.

"Gee," said Ernie. "My pet can't talk, but he'll still win the prize."

Rodeo Rosie rode by on her horse.
"Lance can gallop so fast," she called to
Ernie, "that I know he's going to win
the prize at the show."

"Rufus," Ernie said to the paper bag,
"I know you're not as fast as Lance,
but I still think you'll win the prize."

Meanwhile Oscar was leaning out of his can,
talking to his pet skunk.

"You really smell *yucchy*, Daisy," Oscar said.
"You're going to be the winner at the pet show!"

"Hi, Ernie," said Herry Monster. "Come look at my sweet little kitty. Sam can wash his face with his paw. I'm sure he's going to win the prize at the pet show."

"Gee, Herry, my pet can't wash his face. But I think he's going to win, anyway."

Then Ernie saw Grover and his pet. "Hi, Ernie," said
Grover. "Look at my furry little puppy, Floyd. He is
sooo cute and adorable, I just know he will win the
prize!"

Ernie sat down in the playground swing.

"Gee," he said to himself. "My pet can't coo, can't swim, can't talk, can't gallop, can't wash his face, and he isn't even furry...."

Meanwhile the Count was busy getting his pet ready for the pet show. "Hold still, Octavia. I want to tie a ribbon on each of your lovely arms! There…that's one arm…two arms…three…stop wiggling, Octavia, darling! Four, five, six, seven, *eight*! Eight beautiful arms! Surely you will win the prize."

When Ernie saw Betty Lou, she was coaching her
pet frog.
    "Come on, Louise. You can hop higher than that!"
she said. "Oh, hi, Ernie. Look what Louise can do.
I bet she'll win the prize at the pet show."

"Is everybody ready?" said Sherlock Hemlock, who
was the judge. "The Sesame Street Pet Show is about to
begin!"

Judge Sherlock Hemlock moved slowly down the
line, looking carefully at every pet.

"Egad!" said Sherlock as he watched Goldie swim
a lap.

"Eight arms? Incredible!" he remarked as he
examined Octavia the Octopus.

"Cute and furry indeed!" he said, inspecting Grover's
puppy, Floyd.

"Ahem! I have made up my mind!" announced
Sherlock.

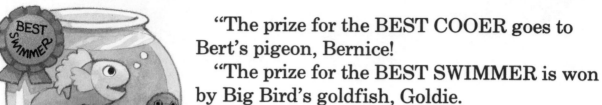

"The prize for the BEST COOER goes to Bert's pigeon, Bernice!

"The prize for the BEST SWIMMER is won by Big Bird's goldfish, Goldie.

"Cookie Monster's parrot, Patricia, wins the prize for BEST TALKER, and Rodeo Rosie's horse, Lance, wins the prize for BEST RUNNER!

"Daisy, Oscar's skunk, wins SMELLIEST, and Sam, Herry's kitten, wins CLEANEST.

"Grover's puppy, Floyd, is definitely the FURRIEST pet. Octavia the Octopus, the Count's pet, wins the prize for MOST ARMS, and Betty Lou's frog, Louise, wins the BEST HOPPER prize.

"Everyone's pet is special," said Sherlock Hemlock. "Everyone's pet wins a prize!"

"Wait!" cried Ernie. "You haven't seen *my* pet yet!"

Ernie took a glass jar out of his brown paper bag. The top of the jar had holes punched in it. He unscrewed the top and dumped out a small bug.

"This is Rufus," said Ernie.

"That's your pet?" asked Betty Lou. "A little bug?"

"Don't tell me that boring bug is your terrific pet!" said Oscar.

"What kind of prize can your bug win, Ernie?" asked Big Bird.

Then Rufus began to glow.
"Oh, my goodness!" shouted
Grover. "He lights up!"
"To Rufus the Firefly," said
Sherlock Hemlock, "I award the
prize of BRIGHTEST PET!"
"Hooray!" shouted everyone.